MATT CHRISTOPHER

On the Mound with...
Randy Johnson

Little, Brown and Company
Boston   New York   Toronto   London

First Edition

Library of Congress Cataloging-in-Publication Data

Christopher, Matt.
    Randy Johnson / Matt Christopher. — 1st ed.
      p.   cm.
    Summary: A biography of the unusually tall pitcher who became a
baseball star for the Seattle Mariners.
    ISBN 0-316-14221-2
    1. Johnson, Randy, 1963–   — Juvenile literature. 2. Baseball
players — United   States — Biography — Juvenile   literature.
    [1. Johnson, Randy, 1963– . 2. Baseball players.] I. Title.
GV865.J599C57   1998
796.357'092 — dc21
[B]   97-32500

10 9 8 7 6 5 4 3 2 1

COM-MO

Contents

MATT CHRISTOPHER

On the Mound with...

Randy Johnson

Chapter One
1963–1977

Big Dreams in Little League

ZIP!

The time it takes to read that word is the amount of time it takes Randy Johnson's ninety-seven-mile-per-hour fastball to reach home plate. A major league hitter has just over one third of a second to decide where the ball is going and take a swing at it.

ZIP!

The Seattle Mariner Johnson is one of the best pitchers in major league baseball today and one of the hardest-throwing pitchers in the history of the game.

Over the last several seasons, he has been almost unbeatable, averaging more than eleven strikeouts per nine innings. He has thrown a no-hitter, led his team to baseball's postseason playoffs, and struck out as many as nineteen batters in a single game, a major league record for a left-handed pitcher.

When Randy stands on the mound and glares in at the hitter, his long hair and mustache make him look intimidating. "When I'm pitching," he says, "I'm a warrior." Yet off the field he is friendly, the father of two small children.

At six feet ten inches tall, Johnson is the tallest person ever to play major league baseball. That's why he is nicknamed "The Big Unit." Opposing managers sometimes bench their left-handed-hitting batters, rather than have them face Johnson. Many batters are afraid to hit against him. A few players even find excuses not to play when Randy is on the mound.

When he winds up and throws the ball, he is so big that he looks as if he is much closer to home plate than other pitchers are. In fact, his arms and legs are so long and his windup is so unusual that he actually releases the ball closer to home plate and from a different angle than any other pitcher. The ball often looks as if it is going to hit the lefty batter until the last instant, when it streaks over the corner of the plate for a strike.

But there is a lot more to Randy Johnson than size and his overpowering fastball. Success did come easily to Randy Johnson. A good fastball, even one as fast as Randy Johnson's, isn't enough to guarantee that someone can be a winning pitcher in the major leagues.

Pitching is more than just throwing the ball fast. Most major league hitters can hit even a hundred-mile-per-hour fastball if they anticipate it is coming and it is thrown down the middle of the plate. Even with a good fastball, a pitcher still must learn to throw several other pitches, and throw the ball to certain spots where it is difficult to hit.

Yet even that is not enough to ensure success. A pitcher must also learn to stay focused and not get flustered when a batter does get a hit or a fielder makes an error. A good pitcher is constantly making adjustments and thinking about the next pitch, no matter what happened to the last one. All he cares about is winning the game.

Johnson wasn't born with the ability to throw one hundred miles an hour. He spent years learning to harness his natural talent and throw the ball where he wanted to. Even when he did, he still had to learn to control his own emotions. Only then did he begin to fulfill his potential and become one of the best pitchers in baseball.

Randy was born in Walnut Creek, California, on September 10, 1963, to Carol and Rollen Johnson. In a family that included five other children, Randy was the baby.

When Randy was still young, the family moved to nearby Livermore, California, a small city southeast of San Francisco.

Randy's father, Rollen, was known as "Bud" to his friends. He was a big, strong man. He stood six feet six inches tall and worked as a police officer. All of Randy's brothers were tall too.

Randy was no exception. He grew quickly, and by the time he entered school, he was one of the tallest children in his class.

It was difficult for Randy to be so tall. He was also very skinny, and other kids sometimes made fun of him. In an effort to become more popular, Randy became the class clown.

While the other kids enjoyed his antics, Randy's teachers did not. He once told a reporter, "I was in the principal's office a lot because I was kind of loud in the classroom, making jokes and disrupting the class."

Randy's parents knew his size was the reason behind his trouble. At home, they were strict with their son. They knew that if he was ever going to make something of his life, he would have to learn to control himself.

After school, Randy turned his attention toward sports. Bud had been a good athlete, and he encouraged Randy to play sports as much as he wanted. In most sports, size was an asset. Bud knew that playing sports could help Randy build self-confidence and learn to become comfortable with himself.

Randy played just about everything. His brothers often let him tag along to the schoolyard and parks. He also rode motocross bikes and traveled all around town on his skateboard. For a while, he played tennis almost every chance he had.

Randy soon discovered he was best at basketball and baseball. On the basketball court, Randy could easily shoot the ball over smaller players and grab rebounds. And in baseball, his long arms and legs enabled him to throw a ball much faster than most boys his age.

Yet Randy's baseball career nearly ended before it even started. He joined Little League, and after practicing with his team a few times, looked forward to their first game. But he misunderstood his coach and arrived at the complex of baseball fields late, then couldn't find his team. He ran back home in tears, certain that he would not be allowed back on the team.

Of course he was. He threw the ball better than anyone else on his team and became a pitcher. Because he was so tall — by the age of twelve, he was nearly six feet tall! — and threw the ball so fast, batters were afraid to hit against him. Yet although Randy threw hard, he had very little control. He usually didn't know where the ball was going.

Randy enjoyed pitching. Standing on the mound with the ball in his hand, it felt good when his teammates yelled, "Go get 'em, Randy. Strike this guy out!" Then he would rear back and throw the ball as hard as he could. On the baseball diamond, no one teased Randy Johnson about his height for long.

While growing up, Randy never even thought about playing major league baseball someday. He just wanted to improve because playing well made him feel good about himself.

In between games he often practiced pitching at home, throwing a tennis ball against the garage for hours, trying to get the ball to go where he wanted it to.

Bud was the first person to realize that his son might have a special talent. One day he noticed that some of the boards on the side of the garage were coming loose. He took a closer look and saw that the nails were popping out. Randy was throwing the ball so hard that the building was slowly coming apart!

Bud didn't want his garage to fall down, but he also didn't want his son to stop practicing a sport that he enjoyed so much. So he simply drove the nails back in. After that, he checked the condition of the garage every few weeks, made the necessary repairs, and told Randy to keep on throwing.

Bud also told his son that if he kept practicing, he might someday reach the major leagues. Randy was flabbergasted. As he remembered later, "No one else ever sat me down and said, 'You've got all the potential in the world.' My dad did that." He enjoyed playing, but hadn't realized before that he had the talent to play professionally. He began to take baseball a little more seriously.

Now when he threw the ball up against the garage wall, he pretended that he was in the major leagues. He would imagine that he heard the public address announcer say, "Now pitching, Randy Johnson!" and the crowd would start cheering. Then a great hitter like Reggie Jackson or George Brett would step into the batter's box.

He often imagined the same game situation. With his team ahead by only a run, Jackson or some other hitter would step up to the plate with a chance to win the game with a home run.

Randy would glare in at the imaginary hitter. Then he would slowly wind up and throw at a spot on the garage wall.

ZIP!

"Stee-rike three!" the umpire would yell. For an instant, Randy could imagine Jackson taking a big cut, missing the ball completely, then storming back toward the dugout as Randy's teammates ran from the dugout and lifted him to their shoulders. He had won the game for them again!

Now Randy knew what he wanted to do with his life. He had a goal.

He wanted to pitch in the major leagues.

Chapter Two
1978–1982

High School Hurler

When Randy entered Livermore High School in the ninth grade, he was well over six feet tall. As a freshman, he played both basketball and baseball on the junior varsity teams. Although he was talented in both sports, he wasn't a big star.

When Randy was in tenth grade, he hoped to play varsity basketball. But the varsity basketball coach had a rule that everyone on the team had to be able to run a mile in less than seven minutes. Try as he might, Randy just couldn't do it. He ran well for short periods of time, but he was so tall and gangly, he just didn't yet have enough stamina to run a mile so quickly.

Despite the fact that he was still growing and had been one of the best players in ninth grade, he was cut from the team. At first, Randy was crushed.

But instead of getting down on himself, he turned his attention back to baseball. That spring he again tried out for the baseball team. Once more he made the junior varsity squad.

Although he threw fast, he still didn't always know where the ball was going. Nevertheless, he usually pitched well enough to win, often striking out ten or eleven batters in a single game.

The opposing team sometimes tried to rattle Randy and make him lose his concentration. They'd call him names that poked fun at his height and looks, like "long-necked geek." Randy tried to ignore their jeers and concentrate on pitching, but once in a while he allowed their taunts to get under his skin.

When that happened, Randy got all worked up and tried to throw the ball even harder than normal. Then he usually lost his control completely and started walking batter after batter. The coach would remove him from the game.

As he recalled later, as he grew above six feet tall, "I started getting noticed a lot because of my height. I felt like I was in a three-ring circus and didn't know how to handle it." When Randy would go to hang out at the local mall with his friends, he felt like a freak and was certain people were talking about him behind his back. "It was hard growing up," he admits today.

Randy probably didn't realize it then, but his body was still growing. As it did, it was hard for him to retain his coordination. That was part of the reason why he felt so awkward and had a hard time throwing strikes. Like all teenagers, he was also struggling to make the transition from childhood to adulthood. Learning to control your emotions is part of that transition.

At the end of his sophomore year Randy was promoted to the varsity baseball team for a big tournament. He pitched well, and the other baseball coaches in the East Bay Athletic Conference began to take notice of the big pitcher from Livermore.

In his junior year Randy tried out for the basketball team again, but he still couldn't run the mile as fast as the coach wanted him to. He again turned his attention back to baseball.

The Livermore Cowboys had a new baseball coach, Eric Hoff. Hoff had heard all about Johnson from other coaches in the league and was excited at the prospect of having him as a pitcher on the team.

Randy hadn't stopped growing. He now stood nearly six feet nine and weighed about 180 pounds. His fastball kept getting faster, and he occasionally threw over ninety miles per hour.

Very few high school batters can hit a ball thrown ninety miles per hour. But Coach Hoff knew that if Randy was going to play baseball after high school, he would have to learn to throw other pitches. Throwing hard just wasn't enough. He had to learn to pitch. "He definitely had a lot of talent, a live arm," remembered Hoff later. "He didn't have the mentality of a pitcher but he had the tools."

Hoff tried to get Randy to think like a pitcher, instead of just being someone who threw the ball toward the plate without any idea of where it was going. He encouraged Randy to throw his curveball and helped him develop a change-up, a pitch that looks just like a fastball when it leaves the pitcher's hand but is actually much slower. When the pitch is thrown for a strike, it upsets the hitter's timing.

Randy worked hard and made sure to mix in a few

curveballs and change-ups. He began to improve. Soon he was in command in nearly every game, giving up only three or four hits and striking out ten or eleven batters.

But Randy's team wasn't very good and didn't score many runs. Even though Randy pitched well, he lost as many games as he won. It seemed as if every mistake the Cowboys made cost Randy a run. Someone would make an error, then Randy would walk a batter, then the next hitter would fight off a good pitch and slice the ball just fair down the line for a base hit. One streak of bad luck was often enough to cost Randy a win.

Randy was frustrated, but he didn't take it out on his teammates. If anything, he blamed himself.

Talking with his father helped. Bud attended nearly every game and afterward would talk to his son for hours. "I got more help from him sometimes than I did from the coaches," remembered Randy. Bud helped Randy understand that there were some things, like errors and the inability of his team to score runs, that he couldn't control. All he could do was try to throw strikes and give his team a chance to win.

Despite the fact that Randy had trouble winning, it didn't take long for college coaches and professional scouts to hear about the giant pitcher from Livermore who threw the ball ninety miles an hour. With each game Randy played, more and more scouts showed up to watch him. They would sit behind the backstop, a notebook and a radar gun in their hands, and keep track of every pitch that Randy threw.

Already, he was as tall as anyone who had ever played in the major leagues. Yet of all the pitchers as tall as Randy who had ever played major league baseball, only a few had ever been very successful. The taller a pitcher is, the more difficulty he often has with his windup and delivery, what scouts and coaches call "mechanics." To succeed, a pitcher must throw exactly the same way each and every time. It's hard for a tall pitcher to do that.

To the professional baseball scouts and college coaches, Randy was an intriguing prospect. Scouts usually prefer big pitchers because they have the potential to throw harder than smaller players. Randy was certainly big. But at the same time, he was so big they wondered if he would ever be able to control the ball well enough to succeed. As one scout commented about Randy, "I never liked to draft guys taller than six foot five. It's tough for them to get everything together." The scout worried that Johnson "never threw the ball twice from the same release point. I didn't know if he'd ever get his mechanics straightened out."

Although Randy was becoming a big baseball star, he didn't act that way at school. He had a few close friends, but he wasn't the most popular guy. He was into heavy metal music and played the drums. Pounding away on the drums as hard as he could helped release some energy. And although he didn't realize it, playing the drums helped his hand-eye coordination, too.

Sometimes he and his friends would get a bunch of guitars and amplifiers together and play music in someone's basement. They never formed a real band, but they kept practicing anyway. It was fun, and helped Randy to relax.

Whenever he needed pocket money, Randy usually found a job cutting grass or doing yard work for neighbors. Even though Randy played summer baseball for a team in the Connie Mack League and couldn't take a regular part-time job, Bud and Carol Johnson made sure he knew the value of work.

In Randy's senior year at Livermore High, the school hired a new basketball coach. He thought the mile-run requirement was silly.

Randy ran to see Coach Hoff. "Coach," he said, "is it OK if I try out for basketball again this year? I think I can make the team."

Hoff just laughed. Even though he worried that his star pitcher might get hurt playing basketball, he thought students should play as many sports as they wanted. "Go ahead," he told him, "but don't forget about baseball."

This time, Randy made the team easily. He played center and became a star as he finally began to gain some control over his body. In one game, he scored fifty-one points! Randy led his league in scoring and was named to the league and regional all-star team.

When basketball season ended, baseball season started. As he began his final year of high school baseball, he had a decision to make. Professional scouts and college coaches were still interested in him. He was certain to be drafted by a major league team in the free-agent draft later that spring. But he was also certain to be offered a scholarship to play baseball or basketball in college. He had to decide what to do.

Randy and his parents met with Coach Hoff several times to discuss his future. Basketball was out. Randy wanted to play baseball. As Hoff remembers, they decided that unless a major league team made Randy an overwhelming offer, it was more important to get Randy into school. Hoff knew Randy had the ability to play in Division I, the highest classification in college sports, so they ignored inquiries from Division II or III schools. Although Randy's parents worried that their son might have difficulty with the coursework in college, Hoff assured them that he could succeed. Randy was only a B and C student, but had the potential to do much better.

Nothing Randy did during his final year of high school baseball made either the pro scouts or college coaches less interested in him. He had matured into a fine all-around athlete, and was actually better coordinated than most high school students his age. When he didn't pitch, he played center field and was one of the best hitters on the team.

But Randy's future was on the pitcher's mound. He pitched well all season long, striking out as many as sixteen batters in a single game and earning MVP honors in several important tournaments. Each time he pitched, there were more and more scouts in the crowd. They often clocked his fastball at ninety-three miles per hour, faster than many major league pitchers!

Randy wasn't the only talented player in his league, either. Two opponents, catcher Mike Mac-farlane and infielder Lance Blankenship, went on to play in the major leagues. Several others eventually played minor league ball.

In his final high school game, and with no less than twenty major league scouts crowded around the backstop and several college coaches in the crowd, Randy demonstrated that he was something special. For all seven innings he shut down the opposing team, sending thirteen batters back to the bench dragging their bats, strikeout victims of Randy's overpowering fastball. Not a single batter collected a hit, and for the first time in his high school career, Randy didn't even walk one person. In fact, no one on the other team even reached first base.

Randy Johnson pitched a perfect game! It was a great way to end his high school career. He finished his senior year with 121 strikeouts in 66⅓ innings.

Several weeks later, Randy was drafted in the third round by the Atlanta Braves. That meant that of all the players in high school and college eligible to be drafted by the major leagues, Randy was considered one of the sixty or seventy best. At the same time, he was offered a full scholarship to play baseball for the University of Hawaii, a Division I school.

Coach Hoff and the Johnsons carefully considered the two offers. Although the Braves offered Randy a sixty-thousand-dollar bonus to turn pro, Hoff and Randy's parents worried that he wasn't mature enough for professional baseball. Playing minor league baseball was hard, and they weren't sure if Randy was ready. He sometimes still got all worked up over things he couldn't control and struggled with feeling self-conscious because of his height. They were afraid that if he didn't succeed immediately in pro ball, he might get frustrated. Besides, they believed a college education was worth more than sixty thousand dollars.

Randy agreed. As he later told a reporter, "I'd

seen too many of my friends sign [out of high school] and then get hurt." Going to college made more sense. If he got hurt or didn't make it to the major leagues, a college degree would help him get a good job. Besides, after three years of college Randy would once again become eligible for the professional draft. The next time around, it was possible that he would be picked in the first or second round and be offered a better contract.

Just as Randy was about to accept the offer from the University of Hawaii, several other colleges expressed interest in him. College baseball powerhouses like the University of Arizona and Arizona State University both wanted Randy.

Then, at the last minute, Randy was contacted by the University of Southern California. Coach Rod Dedeaux had been with the team for over forty years and the USC Trojan baseball program was one of the best in the country. A number of major leaguers, like Hall of Fame pitcher Tom Seaver, and slugger Mark McGwire, had graduated from Dedeaux's program and gone on to successful careers in the big leagues.

It seemed like the perfect situation for Randy, but

there was just one catch. USC only offered Randy a partial *basketball* scholarship. Although they wanted him to attend the school to play baseball, they didn't want to give him a full scholarship. The basketball team had a partial scholarship available, and agreed to give it to Randy with the understanding that he could work out with the basketball team in the fall and play baseball in the spring. If Randy played well, he might earn a full scholarship later.

Although Coach Hoff thought USC was the perfect school for Randy to attend, he didn't think much of the offer. After all, Randy was one of the best baseball prospects in the country. With the Johnsons' permission he told USC that unless Randy received a full scholarship, for baseball only, he would attend the University of Hawaii.

USC finally agreed to offer Randy a full scholarship, just for baseball. Randy and his family decided to accept.

The prospect was off to college. Bud Johnson's garage would survive.

Chapter Three
1982–1985

The Trojan

Randy began college in the fall of 1982. He could hardly believe how much different it was from high school.

In Livermore, Randy had known just about everyone. But at USC, in Los Angeles, there were thousands and thousands of students. Everyone was a stranger and Randy was still self-conscious about the way he looked.

Classes were more difficult, too. Randy had never studied very hard in high school. Now he had to study for hours almost every night.

Baseball was also a struggle. USC played in both a fall league and the regular spring season. Randy had to adjust to being away from home, adapt to college-level academics, and play baseball, all at the same time.

At first, he struggled. He was homesick, having trouble in his classes, lonely, and trying to absorb all the advice he got from the Trojan coaching staff. Then, after pitching only seventeen innings in the fall, he developed a sore arm. Randy was a little overwhelmed.

But after a few months, Randy started to adjust. He made new friends and began to feel at home. With help from a tutor and some of his teachers, he learned how to study and keep up with his schoolwork. He rested his arm, and it soon stopped hurting. Now all he had to do was figure out how to throw strikes and win baseball games.

The Trojan baseball program was in transition. Despite the school's past record of success, the 1983 Trojan team was coming off a sixth-place finish in the Pacific Coast Conference, the worst performance since Dedeaux began coaching the team in 1942.

That worked to Randy's advantage. Freshman athletes often have to wait a year or two before getting much playing time. But the Trojans needed pitching help. Randy got to pitch right away.

The biggest change Randy noticed between high

school and college baseball was the size of the strike zone. Even though the rules state that the strike zone is the space over home plate that is between the batter's armpits and the top of the knees, in reality the zone varies between different levels of play and individual umpires. In high school, the strike zone is often quite large, a fact that helped Randy.

But in college most umpires used a much smaller zone. Chest-high pitches that were called strikes in high school were balls in college baseball. In fact, it was hard to get a strike called on any pitch more than two or three inches above the batter's waist.

In his freshman year, Randy was used primarily as a relief pitcher, coming into the game after the starting pitcher had tired. He finished the year with five wins and three saves, but struck out only thirty-four hitters in forty-seven innings. His earned run average, the average number of runs a pitcher gives up per every nine innings, was over five. Under two is considered great, under three very good, and under four is OK. An ERA above five isn't very good.

Randy's problem was that he was afraid to walk hitters. The small strike zone intimidated him. Instead of throwing the ball freely, he "short-armed" the ball, aiming his pitches in an attempt to throw more strikes. That helped his control a little, but at the expense of his speed. His fastball rarely topped ninety miles per hour. The big prospect was turning suspect.

As Randy struggled, he sometimes grew frustrated. He would get so intense that several innings after making a bad pitch he would still be muttering to himself about it. Sometimes when the ball was hit, Randy would race over to first base and make calls just like the umpire. In between pitches he sometimes talked to the baseball and yelled at the hitters. His teammates thought Randy was a real character.

What Randy didn't realize was that his antics caused him to expend energy uselessly and made him lose his concentration. Professional scouts, who were now following Randy in college, began to be concerned. When they looked at Randy they saw a player with a world of potential but worried that he might never be able to calm down enough to take full advantage of his ability.

In his sophomore year, more familiar with college and college-level play, Randy began to settle down.

He stopped aiming the fastball and began to throw freely. Once again his fastball began zipping to the plate at more than ninety miles per hour.

The Trojan coaching staff began using Randy as a starting pitcher. He had too much potential to use in relief. They wanted him to pitch as much as he could.

Randy responded well. He pitched 78 innings and gave up only 72 hits with a record of 5–3. Although he was still wild, and walked 52 batters, he also struck out 73. His earned run average dropped to 3.35. The Trojans finished in a tie for second place in the PCC and made the postseason College World Series tournament, where they lost in the first round.

Pro scouts were ecstatic. Although they still worried about his streaks of wildness, Randy was beginning to fill out and now weighed nearly two hundred pounds. He added several miles per hour to his fastball.

He was doing better at school, too. Randy discovered that he enjoyed taking art classes and became a fine arts major. He specialized in photography, and he became a familiar face around campus, a six-feet-ten-inch giant with a camera constantly hanging around his neck.

Entering his junior year, Randy was optimistic. His performance as a sophomore made him one of the hottest baseball prospects in the country. It appeared as if he was finally getting it together and that he would be picked in the first round of the pro draft. All he had to do was keep improving.

Randy began his junior year as the ace of the Trojan pitching staff. He believed that it was going to be his year and looked forward to winning ten or eleven games.

But after their second-place finish in 1984, the 1985 Trojans were never able to put it together. Their relief pitching was inconsistent, and they had a hard time scoring enough runs to win. Team spirit was dismal. It was his high school baseball career all over again.

Randy pitched well, but he couldn't win all by himself. He usually led until late in the game, when he tired. Then he either lost control or the USC bullpen collapsed.

That's what happened in one early-season contest against the University of California at Santa Bar-

bara. Randy entered in the ninth inning leading 2–1. He gave up a leadoff walk and then a single, and was pulled from the game in favor of a relief pitcher. But the relief pitcher gave up a walk and double. Since a player Randy put on base scored the winning run, Randy was charged with the loss. In at least three other games, Randy left with a lead only to watch in dismay as his bullpen lost the game.

Even when that didn't happen, Randy sometimes allowed himself to be affected by the lack of support he received from his teammates. He felt as if he had to strike out everyone and tried to throw too hard. In a game against Stanford, Randy carried a narrow, 4–3 lead through five innings and appeared in command. But in the sixth, he tried to be too perfect. He opened the inning by walking the first five batters and lost the game.

"It's frustrating," Randy later admitted to a reporter. "I'm throwing better this season, but I'm pitching in spurts. I'm not consistent like you have to be in pro ball. I'm giving up too many walks and you can't do that."

With an 11–5 win over the University of California in the last game of his junior year, Randy finished with a record of 6–9 and a 5.32 ERA. But if his bullpen had done the job, he may well have finished with nine or ten wins and an ERA much closer to four. In 118 innings of work, he struck out 99 batters. But he walked 104. The Trojans finished the season with their worst record ever and didn't qualify for postseason play.

Yet most pro scouts weren't put off. They agreed with Randy's own self-assessment and felt that with the proper instruction, his control would improve. After all, they reasoned, there just aren't many prospects who can throw the ball as hard as Randy. They figured his potential was worth taking a chance on.

The magazine *Baseball America,* which covers collegiate and minor league baseball, rated Randy as the twelfth-best prospect in the country, and the fourth-best pitcher. In the upcoming draft, many observers expected Randy to be chosen in the first round.

When draft day arrived in early June, Randy was both excited and anxious. He was eager to begin his professional career, and wondered which team would draft him and when.

Finally, Randy received a call from an official of the Montreal Expos. The Expos had drafted Randy in the second round.

For a split second, Randy was disappointed. He had been looking forward to being picked in the first round. Slipping to the second round would probably cost him about one hundred thousand dollars in bonus money.

Then he got excited. After all, he was going to be a professional baseball player. He was moving closer to his goal.

Chapter Four
1985–1988

Minor Leagues and Major Problems

In many ways, the Montreal Expos were the perfect major league organization for Johnson to begin his professional career. Over the preceding five or six seasons, the Expos had played well, usually finishing above .500 and challenging for the National League's Eastern Division title. In 1981, when the season was split in half due to a player's strike, the Expos had finished first in the second half and made the playoffs, where they lost a hard-fought series to the Los Angeles Dodgers, who eventually defeated the New York Yankees in the World Series.

The Expos organization had a fine reputation throughout baseball. They had one of the best minor league systems in the game. They didn't rush prospects to the majors, and were known for their patience and ability to teach younger players. Most of the players on the major league team had been developed in the Expos minor league system.

That was just what Randy needed. Privately, many scouts believed that Johnson hadn't received the proper instruction at USC. With the program struggling, the coaching staff hadn't been able to afford to remake Randy's motion and take the chance that he would struggle for a while. So, even after three years of college ball, he still threw much the same way he had in high school. His control had barely improved in college.

Every major league team has a system of minor league teams that they use to develop players. Each minor league is classified so players perform against players of similar ability and experience. The lowest classification is called a "rookie" league. In order of difficulty, other leagues are classified as "single A," "double A," or "triple A." If a player is good enough to succeed in triple A, his next stop is the major leagues.

Johnson was still a long way from reaching the major leagues. He signed a contract for a substantial bonus and the Expos assigned him to their single-A minor league team in Jamestown, New York, a small city in western New York near Buffalo. Most players in the New York–Pennsylvania League were just beginning their pro careers.

The toughest part about breaking into professional baseball usually has little to do with what goes on during the games. The adjustment to living on your own in a strange city and adapting to minor league life is often a greater challenge.

When Randy started his pro career, most minor league players earned less than one thousand dollars a month. Because players are never sure how long they'll remain in their home city, they usually share small apartments or stay in rooming houses. When they go on the road, they must travel for hours in cramped buses and stay in cheap motel rooms. Many otherwise talented athletes simply can't adjust to the hardships of minor league life.

Although Randy's bonus money made him comfortable financially, that didn't help him much when the team went on the road. Bus travel is uncomfortable even for people of average height, and most motels don't have beds made for people six feet ten inches tall.

Randy hoped to pitch well enough for Jamestown that he would be promoted to another team before the end of the season. He had one definite reason for thinking that possible. For the first time in his life he would get to pitch against players using wooden bats. In college and high school, batters used aluminum.

The difference is dramatic. It's easier to hit with aluminum bats. Balls hit off the fists can still make the outfield for base hits. The same hit off a wooden bat usually results in a weak ground ball or a broken bat. For a hard thrower like Johnson, wooden bats can result in five or six fewer hits per game.

But at the same time, competition in the minor leagues is much better. Nearly every player in minor league ball was a star in high school or college.

Unfortunately, Johnson hardly had the chance to find out how he stacked up against the competition. Almost as soon as he arrived in Jamestown, he came down with a sore arm. The Expos wanted to make sure he didn't hurt himself permanently, and for the rest of the season he hardly pitched. Even when he did, the results weren't impressive.

Johnson finished the season with an 0–3 record in eight games. He did strike out 21 in only 27⅓ innings, but he walked 24. His ERA was 5.93.

Johnson was disappointed, but his brief debut had taught him a few things. He now knew, more than ever, that he had to learn to become a pitcher. He also realized that he had to get in better shape. His arm was simply worn out after pitching just over one hundred innings for USC.

He worked out hard in the off-season, and when he reported to Florida for spring training in March of 1986, he had added twenty pounds of muscle. He was no longer skinny, but powerful and strong.

Johnson impressed the Expos at their minor league training camp. For the 1986 season they assigned him to play for West Palm Beach in the Florida State League. While still an A League, the FSL is considered to be faster than the New York–Pennsylvania League. Many FSL players have already played a year or two in the minors.

Johnson got off to a quick start. Thanks to his hard work in the off-season, his arm felt fine and he was throwing the ball better than he ever had in his life.

Most batters in the FSL had never faced a pitcher

like Johnson. While they may have faced pitchers who threw above ninety miles per hour, they had never seen a pitcher who released the ball from where Randy did.

A left-hander, Johnson's long arms and legs allow him to release the ball far to the first-base side of the pitcher's mound. His natural motion is almost sidearm. So instead of the ball coming straight in at the hitter, the ball comes from an entirely different angle.

As Randy explains, "The trajectory I have throwing downward is different from most pitchers." This is one reason left-handed batters have a particularly hard time hitting against him.

Working with pitching coach Bud Yanus, Johnson's mechanics really started to improve. Instead of viewing Randy's height as a problem to overcome, Yanus saw it as a blessing, and tried to maximize the advantage it gave him. "He probably releases the ball two feet closer to the plate than most pitchers," commented Yanus at the time. That made Johnson's fastball — now being clocked as fast as ninety-seven mph — appear even faster.

Johnson began the season by winning his first six

decisions. Although he was still wild, Yanus noticed, "He's getting better. He doesn't miss with his pitches nearly as bad." The coach taught him a slider, a pitch that looks like a fastball until just before it gets to home plate, when it darts down and away, and kept working with him on a change-up. Johnson was also still adjusting to the professional strike zone, which was even smaller than the one in college ball. Now, it was almost impossible to have a pitch above the waist called a strike. Yet ever so slowly, Randy Johnson was gaining control.

He tired in the second half of the season as cramped bus seats and small motel beds took their toll, but he still finished with an 8–7 record and 133 strikeouts in 119⅔ innings. Better still, his ERA dropped to 3.16. He walked 94 batters, but for Johnson, that was progress.

In 1987 the Expos moved Randy up to their double-A Southern League franchise in Jacksonville. There he was paired with pitching coach Joe Kerrigan.

Unlike Yanus, Kerrigan had pitched in the big leagues. At six feet five, he understood the problems that faced a tall pitcher like Johnson. He continued the work that Yanus had started the previous season.

Most players who sign professional contracts never make it to double-A baseball. Of those that do, most are considered real prospects. If they play well, they have a realistic chance of making it to the big leagues. The Southern League promised to provide a definitive test of Johnson's progress.

He was up to the challenge. While he still walked nearly a hitter an inning, his slider and the location of his fastball improved dramatically. He won eleven games and struck out a league-best 163 batters in only 140 innings. In twenty-five starts, he gave up only one hundred hits.

In the off-season he again worked out hard and added still more muscle. He now weighed 240 pounds.

The added strength paid off in spring training. Johnson was the talk of the Expos camp, where he impressed everyone with his size, his speed, and his surprising command of his pitches.

In many organizations, that performance would have earned him a place with the major league club.

But the Expos were being patient. Even Kerrigan admitted to a reporter at the end of spring training that while Randy was "very, very close" to becoming a major league pitcher, he still lacked consistency. "We are fortunate that at the major league level we have six or seven quality people that could probably start, and I think Randy could use a little more time," he added.

Kerrigan was right. The Expos had won ninety-one games in 1987, primarily on the strength of their pitching staff. There was no need to rush Randy Johnson.

This time he was sent to triple-A Indianapolis of the American Association. In part because of his success with Johnson, Kerrigan was also promoted.

Randy Johnson appeared to be blossoming at just the right time. He began to pitch much more consistently and discovered that triple-A batters found his fastball just as difficult to hit as those in single A or double A had. Many players in triple A had played for a time in the major leagues, so the fact that Randy could still get them out boosted his confidence.

The biggest obstacle that remained was Randy himself. He was still self-conscious. Every time he pitched in Indianapolis he was introduced by the public-address announcer as "the world's tallest pitcher." As he later told a reporter, that "made it sound as if I was a freak," and it bothered him. But he kept his emotions all bottled up inside. Sometimes, he was able to use those feelings in a positive manner while pitching. But on other occasions, they got in the way.

By mid-June, Randy was clearly the best pitcher in the league. Despite his occasional trouble with control, the Expos were convinced that he was ready for the big leagues. On June 14 they decided that after one more start, Randy would join the major league team. They were fighting for the division lead and thought Randy could help.

Johnson was excited but tried to stay focused on his final triple-A start. He was pitching well. Then he threw a fastball that changed everything.

Crack! The hitter got the big part of the bat on the ball and smacked a line drive back at Randy.

Instinctively, Randy reached to block the ball. But

instead of reaching with his glove hand, he blocked the ball with his bare hand.

While the ball rolled to one of his infielders, Johnson collapsed in pain. The ball had hit him on the left wrist, which was already starting to swell. He was certain he had broken it.

Randy couldn't believe it. He had worked so hard and was only hours from jumping on a plane and becoming a big league baseball player. Now his wrist was broken! The only thought that went through his mind was that his career was over.

Johnson was removed from the game and walked disconsolately to the dugout, his head down and his eyes wet with tears.

As he walked past the bat rack on the way to the clubhouse, all the frustrations he had allowed to build up inside himself let go at once. He lashed out and punched the bat rack as hard as he could with his right hand.

Crack! That wasn't the sound of the bat meeting the baseball. It was the sound of his hand meeting the wooden rack. Now *both* hands hurt.

The team sent Randy to the hospital. Doctors took X rays and gave Randy both good and bad news. His left wrist, the one he used to throw a baseball, was merely bruised. In a week he would never know he had been struck. But when he hit the bat rack he had broken a bone in his right hand. He wouldn't be able to play for another six weeks.

The Expos were angry with him. By allowing his emotions to take over, Randy had not only harmed himself, he had hurt Montreal's chances of winning the division.

A few days later the team posted a notice on the bulletin board in the clubhouse of every team in its minor league system. The notice read "ANYBODY WHO DOES SOMETHING HASTY TO INHIBIT HIS ABILITY WILL BE FINED." It was entitled "THE RANDY JOHNSON RULE."

Fortunately for Randy, he healed quickly. By August he was back with his triple-A team and pitching as well as ever. He finished the regular season with an 8–7 record, 3.26 ERA, and 11 strikeouts in 113 innings. Better yet, he walked only 74 batters. That was still a lot, but for Johnson, it was a big improvement.

The Indianapolis Indians won the American Association championship, then defeated the triple-A

Rochester Red Wings of the International League in the postseason playoffs, too. It was nearly mid-September before their season ended.

When it did, Randy finally got the call he had been waiting for. The Montreal Expos promoted Randy to the big leagues.

He had reached his goal. Now, he had to try to stay there.

Chapter Five
1988–1989

Trade Bait

Randy made his debut for the Expos on September 15, 1988, against the Pittsburgh Pirates. While the Expos had fallen out of the race for the divisional title, the Pirates were battling to keep pace with the division-leading New York Mets.

Even though Johnson was one of the most talked about rookies in baseball, only nine thousand fans turned out to see him pitch his first game at Montreal's Olympic Stadium.

The press was more enthusiastic. As soon as he took the mound, Johnson, at six feet ten, would become the tallest person ever to play major league baseball. A pitcher for the Pirates in the 1940s, Johnny Gee, had been six nine.

Before the game the press clamored for Johnson to pose for photographs with several Pirate players who were well under six feet tall. Johnson agreed, but the request disturbed him. He wanted to be seen as a major leaguer, not a circus-sideshow attraction.

When he walked to the mound to begin his major league career, he tried to push those thoughts from his mind. All he wanted to do was throw strikes. Very, very fast strikes.

After escaping the first inning without giving up any runs, Johnson faced Pittsburgh outfielder Glenn Wilson, who led off the second. Johnson then threw a pitch that he wanted back as soon as it left his hand.

Crack! The ball sailed over the left-field fence for a home run. The Expos trailed, 1–0.

Johnson tried not to let the hit bother him. He struck out Orestes Destrade, the next hitter, then induced catcher Junior Ortiz to fly out before striking out shortstop Rafael Belliard for the third out.

The Expos scored three runs in the third inning to take a 3–1 lead. In the fourth inning, Wilson came to the plate again.

This time Randy tried to be too careful. He threw the ball right down the middle of the plate.

Boom! This time Wilson homered to center field. Yet Johnson still led, 3–2.

The Expos scored again to make it 4–2 and Johnson retired the Pirates easily in the fifth inning. When it came time for Randy to bat in the bottom of the inning, the Expos sent up a pinch hitter in his place. Apart from the two home runs, he had pitched well. The team wanted to make sure his first game would be a positive experience for him, so they turned the game over to the bullpen.

The Expos went on to win, 9–4. Randy Johnson was the winning pitcher. In five innings he gave up only two runs on six hits and three walks. He had struck out five batters.

Randy made three more starts, winning two, before the end of the season. In each subsequent appearance he pitched better, exhibiting good control and dominating hitters with his fastball. He finished the season with a record of 3–0 in four appearances, with twenty-five strikeouts and an ERA of 2.42.

The Expos were impressed. He had only walked seven hitters. They planned to have Randy step into the starting rotation in 1989.

He spent the off-season working out in anticipation of the upcoming season. In spring training, he did nothing to indicate that his performance at the end of the 1988 season was a fluke. He dominated hitters, drawing comparisons to some of the great strikeout artists in the history of the game, like Sandy Koufax and Nolan Ryan. The Expos looked forward to a successful year.

They were so optimistic that manager Buck Rodgers announced his pitching staff was "second to none." Star slugger Mike Schmidt of the Philadelphia Phillies was similarly impressed. After getting a look at Johnson and several other pitchers on the Expos staff, he said Montreal "might have the most talented ten-man staff ever." When the team broke camp to begin the season, Montreal fans were already looking forward to the playoffs.

Johnson's strong spring performance earned him the number two spot on the Expos starting staff behind veteran pitcher Dennis Martinez. He made his first appearance as a starter in Montreal's second game of the season. Although he pitched well, he lost to the Pirates, 3–0. But in his next start, against the Phillies, he was wild. Although Johnson didn't get the decision, the Expos lost the game.

In each of his next several starts he struggled with his control. All of a sudden, Randy was walking a batter nearly every single inning.

He just wasn't doing the job. In fact, few of Montreal's pitchers were performing up to expectations. With their record hovering around .500, the Expos grew impatient. "All I know," said manager Buck Rodgers at the time, "is we need leadership from our pitching staff to win and we're not getting it." He was particularly disappointed in Johnson. The team decided they couldn't afford to wait for Randy Johnson to find the strike zone.

In early May, the Expos abruptly sent Johnson back down to minor league Indianapolis. They announced that he would not return to the major leagues until he learned to throw strikes.

Johnson was devastated, but he also understood. He knew he had to throw strikes. In fact, that was just about the only thing he had been thinking about. Yet it seemed as if the more he thought about throwing strikes, the harder it became to do so. He would walk a batter or two, then start aiming the ball and get hit, then try throwing too hard and walk someone again.

Yet as soon as he returned to Indianapolis, he began to relax and throw strikes. It helped that he was able to work once more with pitching coach Joe Kerrigan. Johnson made three starts with Indianapolis and pitched well. He looked forward to returning to the major leagues.

He got his wish, but not with the Expos. All winter long, the Seattle Mariners had made inquiries to the Expos about trading for Johnson, only to be told he was "untouchable." But when they saw Johnson had been demoted to the minor leagues, they sensed that he might now be available in a trade.

On May 25, 1989, the Mariners traded ace left-hander Mark Langston to Montreal for Johnson and two other young pitchers, Brian Holman and Gene Harris.

Langston was considered one of the best pitchers in baseball. But he was scheduled to become a free agent at the end of the season, and it was no secret that he planned to sign with a contending team. By trading him before his contract ran out, the Mariners made certain they received something in return.

The deal satisfied the needs of both clubs. Montreal got the star pitcher they needed, while the Mariners received three players with a great deal of potential.

At first, Johnson was disappointed in the trade. He knew he had let the Expos down and felt bad. But at the same time, he knew he would receive a chance to pitch in Seattle. They were a young team, and needed him to play.

But the deal was not popular in Seattle. The press howled that the Mariners had once again given away a great pitcher for unproven players. Over the past several seasons, they had similarly traded away several other quality starters. More often than not, the prospects they had received in return had bombed.

Johnson was immediately inserted into the Mariners starting rotation. After Langston threw a four-hitter and struck out twelve in his debut with Montreal, Johnson was under plenty of pressure to prove that the deal was a good one for the future of the Seattle franchise.

Johnson joined the team in Milwaukee, where the Mariners were playing the Brewers. His teammates had heard a lot about him, but even they were surprised at the player who arrived in the club-house.

The first thing Johnson did was surround his locker with bright yellow police-barricade tape. Then he pulled a few practical jokes. One favorite was to throw baseballs attached to long strips of adhesive tape to fans in the stands, then pull them back out of reach.

That's simply the way Johnson reacted to the pressures of playing, by acting eccentric and making jokes. There was nothing wrong with any of that as long as he didn't let it get in the way of how he pitched.

Before he even took the mound he let his teammates know he was behind them. In his first game with the team, catcher Dave Valle was bowled over at the plate and Brewers and Mariners players got into a brawl. Johnson himself led the charge from the Seattle bullpen, immediately earning the respect of his teammates for his willingness to back them up. As soon as the Brewers saw Johnson heading their way, the fight stopped.

On May 30, 1989, he took the mound in a Seattle uniform for the first time at Yankee Stadium in New York. The first batter he faced was New York outfielder Rickey Henderson.

The speedy Henderson was the best leadoff hitter in baseball. He crouched way down in the batter's box and as a result had the smallest strike zone in the major leagues. He usually walked well over one hundred times a year.

But if a pitcher tried to aim the ball for a strike, Henderson could make them pay. He had surprising power, and would later set the record for most leadoff home runs in the history of the major leagues.

When Johnson leaned in to get the sign from catcher Scott Bradley, the raucous New York crowd howled. From all corners of the ballpark Johnson heard every possible unkind comment about his height and appearance. He tried to block everything out and concentrate on his task.

He wound up and threw.

Whoosh! The ball zipped past Henderson and exploded into Bradley's mitt.

"Stee-rike!" yelled the umpire. The crowd hushed

and Henderson looked back at the ball in the glove as if he couldn't believe it had gotten there so fast.

It had. And a few pitches later, Johnson had his first American League strikeout.

He went on to pitch six innings, striking out five more hitters and walking only three. Seattle rookie Ken Griffey Jr. cracked two home runs in the Mariners 3–2 victory, and Johnson was credited with the win.

Johnson was subdued after the game. "I was under a microscope," he said, "I had my anxieties. They started when Montreal gave up on me and continued when they traded me.

"I think a lot of people were waiting for me to be wild," he added. "I think I got a lot of first-pitch strikes because they were waiting for me to fall behind. This game was a classic example of how I pitched when I came up at the end of last year."

Johnson's teammates were impressed. First baseman Dave Cochrane told reporters that with Johnson's delivery, it appeared as if he were releasing the ball "nine or ten feet in front of the pitching rubber." Center fielder Ken Griffey Jr. said that from where he was "It looked like he was just handing the ball to the catcher. A couple of innings we didn't even throw our warm-ups. We just stood and watched Johnson."

That's what Seattle fans wanted to hear. They, too, looked forward to watching Johnson.

Chapter Six
1989–1991

Treading Water with the Mariners

Johnson followed his initial victory for the Mariners with several more impressive starts. It appeared as if the control problems that had always plagued him were a thing of the past. In the meantime, although Langston was pitching well, the Expos were going nowhere. The Mariners weren't exactly burning up the Western Division of the American League either, but with Johnson and Ken Griffey Jr., they were optimistic about the future.

Yet as soon as Johnson's control problems appeared to be a thing of the past, they reemerged. By the end of August he couldn't find the plate.

Several poor performances sent his ERA skyrocketing. He won only two of his last nine decisions, and finished the year a disappointing 7–9. Entering

University of Southern California pitcher Randy Johnson throws a mighty fastball.

With a delivery that is almost a sidearm throw, Randy Johnson hurls in a pitch.

Intense concentration plus a rocket left arm are the key factors in the Big Unit's success.

The tallest player in major league baseball gives
a radio interview to a half-pint reporter.

Three Mariners award winners—Lou Piniella, Manager of the Year, Edgar Martinez, Designated Hitter of the Year, and Randy Johnson, Cy Young Award Winner for 1995.

His impressive wingspan is evident as Randy Johnson makes the pickoff attempt at first base.

All-Star starting pitcher Randy Johnson works in the first inning of the 1997 game.

The Big Unit receives high fives from fellow Mariners Ken Griffey Jr. (right) and Jose Cruz Jr. after Johnson helped the team to a 3–0 win against the Toronto Blue Jays in June 1997.

Randy Johnson's Career Highlights

1990:
Member of the American League All-Star Team

1992:
Led the American League in strikeouts (241)

1993:
Led the American League in strikeouts (308)
Member of the American League All-Star Team

1994:
Led the American League in strikeouts (204)
Led the American League in shutouts (4)
Led the American League in complete games (9)
Member of the American League All-Star Team

1995:
Winner of the Cy Young Award
Named *Sporting News* American League Pitcher of the Year
Best ERA in American League (2.48)
Best winning percentage in American League (.900)
Led the American League in strikeouts (294)
Member of the American League All-Star Team

1997:
Posted 20 wins in regular season
Struck out 19 batters in two separate games (a feat that has
  been accomplished only eight times in major league history)
Best winning percentage in American League (.833)
Led American League in strikeouts per nine innings (12.3)
Lowest batting average allowed in American League (.193)
Member of American League All-Star Team

Randy Johnson's Year-to-Year Major League Statistics

Year	Team	Wins	Losses	ERA	Strikeouts	Bases on Balls
1988*	Montreal Expos	3	0	2.42	25	7
1989*	Montreal Expos	0	4	6.67	26	26
1989*	Seattle Mariners	7	9	4.40	104	70
1990	Seattle Mariners	14	11	3.65	194	120
1991	Seattle Mariners	13	10	3.98	228	152
1992	Seattle Mariners	12	14	3.77	241	144
1993	Seattle Mariners	19	8	3.24	308	99
1994	Seattle Mariners	13	6	3.19	204	72
1995	Seattle Mariners	18	2	2.48	294	65
1996†	Seattle Mariners	5	0	3.67	85	25
1997	Seattle Mariners	20	4	2.32	264	73

*Played part of the year in the minors

† Disabled

the 1990 season, Johnson's future was a very large question mark.

Working with Mariners pitching coach Mike Paul, Johnson tried a new approach. Paul admonished him for trying too hard. He felt that if Johnson simply relied on his natural ability, he would do fine. As Paul later recalled, "I used to tell him 'Try easier.' Sometimes when you make it easier, it [the ball] comes quicker."

But it was still difficult for Johnson both to relax and stay focused. His Mariners teammates learned to leave him alone on the days he was scheduled to pitch. He'd work himself into a frenzy. He had grown his hair long and added a Fu Manchu mustache. He could intimidate both his own teammates and the opposition just by the way he looked.

Johnson followed a strict routine before each start that he still follows today. When he gets up in the morning, he eats pancakes, then plays with his dogs and practices the drums, playing along with heavy metal music for an hour. Arriving at the ballpark, he puts on his uniform the same way every day, and stretches and warms up at a specific time.

Yet Johnson still had a difficult time focusing on what was important. Little things bothered him, and on occasion he'd take the mound preoccupied by problems that had nothing to do with baseball. Seattle manager Jim Lefebvre was once asked by a reporter how he expected Randy to pitch in an upcoming game. Responded Lefebvre, "I don't know. It all depends on how well he is getting along with his girlfriend."

Still, Johnson got off to a good start in 1990. Only Seattle's inability to score a lot of runs was preventing him from being a big winner. Then, on June 2, he provided a glimpse of the inspiring feats he would perform more consistently in later years.

One year, one week, and one day after Johnson was traded to the Mariners, he pitched the first no-hitter in the history of the franchise, beating the Detroit Tigers 2–0.

It didn't come easy. Johnson was saved by several fine defensive plays and struggled with his control all night long, walking six hitters. Yet he was able to keep the Tigers hitters off balance.

In the sixth inning, he walked the bases loaded,

but battled back and struck out Chet Lemon to get out of the inning unscathed.

From then on the crowd was on its feet and cheered every pitch. Starting off the ninth, Johnson had to face the Tigers' powerful first baseman Cecil Fielder.

He struck him out. As Fielder said later, "He was throwing that slider for strikes when he was behind in the count, then he comes in with that big fastball. How are you going to hit that? The answer is, you're not and we didn't."

Chet Lemon hit a pop fly for out number two. Up stepped catcher Mike Heath.

Randy quickly went ahead no balls and two strikes. Then he threw a fastball that was even with the batter's shoulders. Heath took a mighty cut and just got a piece of the ball, which he fouled straight back.

Johnson knew this was no time to fool around. Although the slider had been his best pitch for most of the night, there is an old baseball adage that says, "Don't get beat with anything but your best pitch." Johnson decided if he were to lose the no-hitter, he wanted to lose it on his best pitch — his fastball.

He wound up and threw. Heath started to swing before the ball even left Johnson's hand.

It wasn't even close. The pitch streaked past him before he could get his bat around to meet it. The umpire called out "Strike three!" and pumped his right arm in the air.

Johnson was thrilled, but he tried to take his performance in stride. "It was a good no-hitter," he commented later, "but not a great no-hitter." He was well aware of his six walks. He saw no reason to get too worked up over just one game.

Yet the no-hitter made him a household name to baseball fans across the country. A few weeks later, when the American League announced the roster for the All-Star game, Randy Johnson made the team.

He was ecstatic. "I always thought I could be a good major league pitcher," he said, "but I never thought I'd be an All-Star." Even though Johnson didn't appear in the game, with a 9–3 record at the break, he seemed poised to take his place as one of the game's dominant starting pitchers.

But nothing ever seems to come easy to Randy

Johnson. Just when it appeared as if he had put his pitching problems behind him, they emerged again.

He slumped in the second half, struggling with his control for one start, getting hit hard in another, then following up with a game in which he'd be absolutely overpowering, striking out ten or eleven hitters and giving up only a few hits. From one game to the next, it was almost impossible to tell which Randy Johnson was going to take the mound.

He finished with a record of 14–11, a good but not great season. His 120 walks were the most by any pitcher in the American League.

It was more of the same in 1991. Johnson was alternately either horrible or unhittable, and sometimes both horrible and unhittable in the same game. He'd be cruising along, seemingly in total command, when the wheels would suddenly fall off. In a span of twenty or thirty pitches he would go from being one of the best pitchers in baseball to one of the worst. Because he walked so many hitters, and threw so many pitches, he often lost steam late in the game.

In one particularly frustrating outing against the

Milwaukee Brewers, he walked ten batters in only four innings. Yet he still showed flashes of brilliance.

In mid-August he completely baffled the then-powerful Oakland Athletics. With a lineup that featured Jose Canseco and Mark McGwire, two of the best fastball hitters in baseball, Johnson blew them away.

Through the first eight innings of the game, Johnson had it all. His fastball was popping the mitt and his slider was catching the corner. He had walked only a single batter. No one had gotten a base hit.

Nursing a 4–0 lead, Johnson was only three outs away from his second career no-hitter. Then he walked leadoff hitter Scott Brosius.

Light-hitting Mike Gallego was up next. He lined the first pitch into left field for a base hit.

The no-hitter was gone. And Johnson still needed to get three outs in order to win the game.

He fought back to strike out pinch hitter Brook Jacoby for the first out and his tenth strikeout of the game. Rickey Henderson, now with Oakland, was up next.

Henderson walked. All of a sudden the tying run was at home plate!

But Johnson again fought back. He struck out Willie Wilson and the dangerous Canseco to end the game and preserve the shutout for his eleventh win of the season.

He finished 13–10, but his ERA of 3.98 was high for a pitcher of his ability. He did strike out 228 batters, but his 152 walks in just over 200 innings were more than any other pitcher in baseball had allowed. Johnson appeared to be treading water. He was working hard, but not making much progress.

In the off-season the Mariners fired manager Jim Lefebvre and replaced him with Bill Plummer.

Plummer had little patience with Johnson's enigmatic performance. Following a loss to Baltimore on May 26, Plummer complained to the press that Johnson "quit on us and quit on the team." He thought that once Johnson realized he wasn't pitching well or fell behind in a game, he just gave up.

Those words angered Johnson. He was trying as hard as he could, and although he occasionally got frustrated, he never quit.

There was only one way for him to prove that Plummer and his other critics were wrong. He had to start winning.

Chapter Seven
1992

Triumph and Tragedy

No matter how hard he tried in the 1992 season, he continued to struggle. It began to appear as if Randy Johnson would finish his career without ever fulfilling his awesome potential. He was walking as many batters as ever, and his won-loss record was well under .500. In Seattle, there was talk of trading him. The team was simply running out of patience.

In mid-season, the Mariners traveled to Texas to play the Rangers, who were led by their star pitcher, Nolan Ryan.

Although Ryan was of average height, he and Randy Johnson had much in common. Like Johnson, Ryan was blessed with one of the best fastballs in the history of baseball. Early in his career, he too had struggled with his control.

After reaching the big leagues for good with the

New York Mets in 1968, Ryan had spent several seasons both starting and relieving for New York. He threw the ball as hard as anyone in the major leagues, but he rarely knew where it was going. The Mets finally lost patience with him and in 1972 traded Ryan to the California Angels.

Ryan's struggles continued with California. Although he regularly struck out as many as 300 or more hitters in a single season, including a major league record 383 in 326 innings in 1973, he also walked more hitters than any other pitcher in baseball. As a result, his won-loss record hovered around .500.

After being traded to Houston in 1980, Ryan slowly started to gain control of his fastball. But he really got going in 1989, when he joined the Texas Rangers. At an age when most pitchers were ready to retire, Ryan finally put it all together. He learned to throw strikes and spot his pitches without sacrificing speed. After more than twenty years in the major leagues, he had finally figured out how to pitch. No pitcher in the major leagues had ever struck out as many batters as Nolan Ryan.

His pitching coach, Tom House, had provided the

help Ryan needed. House, a former major league pitcher, studied the mechanics of throwing a baseball like a scientist. Working with Ryan, he noticed some tiny mechanical flaws in Ryan's motion. When Ryan learned how to correct those flaws, his control problems disappeared.

When Ryan looked at Randy Johnson, he saw a lot of himself. He knew what Johnson was going through. Even though he played for a different team, Ryan decided to offer Johnson some help.

Ryan and House were working together on an instructional video entitled *FASTBALL*, designed to teach younger players how to throw the ball faster. They contacted Johnson to appear in the video.

The three met in Texas when the Mariners came to play the Rangers. Johnson and Ryan were both in between starts so they had time to work on the video.

Johnson admired Ryan. And although the two had met before, they hadn't had the opportunity really to talk.

Ryan did most of the talking. In the presence of Nolan Ryan, Randy Johnson was definitely the pupil.

Ryan discussed how he set up hitters. Despite having one of the best fastballs ever, Ryan actually got many of his outs with curveballs and change-ups. The key to getting batters out, he explained, was to throw a pitch they don't expect in a place they're not looking.

That wasn't the first time someone had told Johnson that, but hearing those words from Nolan Ryan gave them more credibility. If it worked for Nolan Ryan, reasoned Johnson, it had to work for him.

Then as they began shooting the video, Ryan and House started analyzing Johnson's pitching motion and mechanics. Johnson had worked hard over the years and had made some improvements, but he was still mystified by the way his control would suddenly desert him for no reason.

House and Ryan noticed a couple things. When Johnson got in trouble, he tended to speed up his delivery and start rushing the pitch. Through experience, House and Ryan knew that when a pitcher started rushing, he usually got out of sync and started releasing the ball from a different angle. That made it almost impossible to throw strikes consistently.

House also noticed that when Johnson stepped toward the plate with his right foot during his windup, he landed hard on the heel of his foot. By landing on the heel, his legs weren't able to absorb the impact of his body hurtling toward home plate. Instead, landing on his heel caused his whole upper body to sustain the jolt. In an effort to absorb it, he unconsciously spun toward third base and dropped his arm. From pitch to pitch, the precise position of his arm kept changing. As he tired, the problem usually got worse.

It was no mystery why he wasn't throwing strikes. He rarely threw from the same place twice. Although Johnson had had some good coaching through the years, no one had noticed that subtle flaw.

Ryan and House told Johnson that he should land on the ball of his foot instead. That way, they explained, the impact was absorbed by the arch of his foot, his ankle, and his calf muscles. Instead of spinning toward third at the moment he released the ball, his upper body would remain still and his momentum would carry his arm forward. From pitch to pitch, his release point would stay the same. The result would be better control.

Johnson listened intently. What the two men said made sense. For the first time in his life, he actually began to understand what he had to do to succeed. It wasn't a question of his desire. It was a practical problem, one that House and Ryan had showed him how to overcome.

Now Johnson tried to put their advice into practice. After all, he had nothing to lose. He had just lost eight straight games.

Over the course of his next several starts, his control slowly improved as he tried to implement the changes suggested by Ryan and House. They began to work. Even better, he found that the changes allowed him to throw two or three miles per hour faster! Sometimes his fastball topped out at one hundred miles per hour!

By September, Johnson really started to see results. In one game he struck out fifteen batters, a career high.

His last start of the season was scheduled for September 27 in Texas against the Rangers. The opposing pitcher, also in his last start of the year, was Nolan Ryan.

Johnson was relaxing in the clubhouse before the game when a clubhouse attendant told him he had a telephone call. When Johnson picked up the phone, he was surprised to hear Ryan's voice. Ryan congratulated Johnson on how well he had been pitching and wished him good luck on his final start.

Johnson was impressed. Ryan, at age forty-five, had been battling injuries all year long and had won only five of fourteen decisions. Yet he still thought to call Johnson and wish him good luck.

When Johnson took the mound that night, he had never before felt so comfortable and so confident. Ryan was his idol. The student wanted to prove something to the teacher.

The Ranger offense was one of the best in baseball. Their lineup featured stars like Rafael Palmeiro, Ivan Rodriguez, and sluggers Jose Canseco and Juan Gonzalez. There wasn't an easy out on the team.

Johnson started out strong. With one out in the first, he struck out the next two hitters. His fastball was being timed at ninety-seven or ninety-eight miles per hour, and his slider was darting across the plate with precision.

In the second inning, he struck out the side. In the third, he did it again.

The Texas crowd was roaring. Ryan, while not striking out as many hitters as Johnson, was also pitching well.

Johnson just kept going. After collecting two strikeouts in the fourth, in the fifth and sixth innings, he struck out the side again. After only six innings, he had struck out sixteen of a possible eighteen hitters!

The major league single-game strikeout record is twenty, set by Roger Clemens in 1986. With nine outs remaining, Johnson had a chance to make history!

But in the seventh, he began to tire, and did not strike out a hitter. In the eighth he came back to collect his seventeenth and eighteenth strikeouts.

Although the record was within reach, Johnson was out of gas. The Rangers had scratched out two runs and the game was tied. Johnson, who had walked four hitters, had already thrown 160 pitches.

He asked to be taken out of the game. He didn't

want his pursuit of a record to cost his team the game.

Ryan, too, left with the game tied. But the Mariners scored a single run in the ninth and the bullpen held the lead. Although Johnson didn't get the decision, the Mariners won, 3–2.

Johnson was exhausted but exhilarated after the game. He hadn't matched Clemens's mark, but the eighteen strikeouts tied the American League record for most strikeouts by a left-handed pitcher.

"He brought out the best in me," said Johnson of Ryan when he talked to reporters after the game. "He's what the game is all about. When you face him you have to pitch your best."

Despite the fact that he didn't get the win in his final game, Johnson's strong second half lifted his season record to a respectable 12–14. While he led the league with 144 walks in 210 innings pitched, he also led the American League with 241 strikeouts, the first time he had ever done so.

Randy Johnson entered the off-season more optimistic than ever before. He was convinced that his career had turned the corner. He worked out with weights religiously, trying to build back his strength after a long season. To help his stamina, he ran and rode a bike.

Johnson had finally realized what he had to do to succeed in baseball. But he had done more than learn to control his fastball over the last half of the 1992 season. He had begun to settle down. He had a steady girlfriend, Lisa, whom he soon married. He also renewed his interest in photography, which had waned since his college days.

Wherever the Mariners played, Johnson brought his camera. After games, as he tried to wind down, he usually walked the streets, camera around his neck, looking for photo subjects.

He liked to take pictures that were a little offbeat, like one he took of a compact car that had been placed in a trash bin. Walking around late at night also put him in touch with people less fortunate than he was, like the homeless. Johnson didn't take pictures of them because he didn't want to exploit them. But he sometimes stopped to talk.

Usually, they had no idea who he was. Yet they accepted him, and rarely commented about his size or appearance. Johnson was surprised to learn that he felt he had much in common with such people. Like many of the homeless, Johnson, too, had been made to feel strange and out of place. He admired the people he met for their quiet courage and resiliency.

His contract with the Mariners had expired and Johnson's agent was negotiating a new one. For the first time in his life he would have not only the means but the desire to help others. He promised himself that when he was financially secure, he would give something back to the community.

In December, Johnson signed a one-year contract worth $2.625 million. He would have preferred to sign a longer contract like those the Mariners had just given hitting stars Ken Griffey Jr. and Edgar Martinez, but Seattle wasn't convinced by his late-season turnaround. They wanted to make sure he could do it again before they committed to a longer deal.

Still, as Christmas approached, Johnson had never felt so good. His life was on a steady course. He couldn't wait for spring training.

He and Lisa left their home in suburban Seattle to return to Livermore to spend the holidays with his parents.

But when Johnson arrived home, his world came

crashing down. His father, Bud, had been hospital-ized with heart problems.

Randy rushed to the hospital, but he was too late. Moments before he arrived, Bud Johnson had died.

It was Christmas Day.

Chapter Eight
1993–1995

Strikes and Strikeouts

Randy Johnson was devastated by his father's death. His father had stood beside him for years, building his confidence and telling him everything would work out. Then, just as it appeared that he was right, he was gone. It just didn't seem fair.

Randy asked the doctor if he could spend a final moment with his father. He put his head on his father's chest and cried out, asking, "Why did you have to go now, why now?" There was no answer.

Johnson became deeply depressed. His father had been his best friend. Now, at the time he needed him most, he was gone. There was no one that Randy felt he could talk to about it.

Johnson later admitted, "After he passed away, I seriously thought about giving baseball up. I enjoyed the thrill of telling my dad how good I was on a given night. When he passed away, I realized I had no one to call." There didn't seem to be any reason to keep playing.

Then he realized that was simply being selfish. His father's biggest dream was for Randy to become a great major league pitcher. While he had reached the major leagues, he had not fulfilled his father's dream. Now, he promised himself he would.

When Johnson arrived at spring training, he was a different person. Pitching well was all he cared about. He didn't clown around nearly as much as before, but neither did he get angry or frustrated. He felt as if he had something to prove.

There was a totally different feeling around the Mariners clubhouse, too. Plummer had been let go and replaced by Lou Piniella. An outfielder for the New York Yankees world championship teams in 1977 and 1978, Piniella had since become a successful manager in both New York and Cincinnati. He was tough, but fair, and quickly earned the respect of his players. All Piniella wanted to do was win.

That's what Johnson needed to hear, because that's precisely what he wanted to do.

He began the season pitching just as well as he

had at the end of the 1992 season. While the Mariners staff was decimated by injuries, Johnson held the team together and kept them on the edges of the pennant race. In their entire history, the Mariners had never even finished .500 before.

On May 16, the Mariners played the Oakland Athletics in Oakland, less than an hour drive from where Johnson grew up. It was his first appearance in the Bay Area since his father died.

But Randy had more than his father on his mind. His mother, Carol, was in the hospital, recovering from hip-replacement surgery. Although she was in no danger, the game would be the first Johnson had ever pitched so close to home without either of his parents in the stands.

Seattle hadn't won a game in Oakland since 1990. Although the A's weren't quite the powerhouse they had been then, they remained a good-hitting team. Slugger Mark McGwire was hurt, but the A's lineup still featured Rickey Henderson and Ruben Sierra.

All that mattered little to Randy Johnson. He went to the mound ready to prove his worth.

From the first pitch of the game, he was dominant. The A's didn't have a chance.

On virtually every hitter, he threw the first pitch for a strike, giving him an advantage he had only rarely enjoyed in the past. That caused the A's hitters to become defensive. Once they did, Johnson took command.

If they looked for the slider, Johnson threw a fastball. When they looked fastball, he threw either a slider or a change-up. Even when they guessed correctly, Johnson's fastball was so quick it shot past them before they even got their bat off their shoulder.

As Oakland manager Tony LaRussa said after the game, "He could have played the '72, '73, '74 A's and you would have seen the same result," referring to the A's world championship teams of two decades earlier. Johnson was that dominant.

He had a perfect game, meaning no batter had reached base, until one out in the eighth inning. Then Kevin Seitzer walked, only to be erased on a double play moments later.

Meanwhile, the Mariners had scored seven runs. Entering the ninth inning, Johnson had still faced the minimum number of hitters.

Mike Bordick led off for Oakland. He worked Johnson for a walk.

Then Terry Steinbach hit a ground ball. Bordick was forced out, but Steinbach reached first base on the fielder's choice. Johnson's no-hitter was intact.

Lance Blankenship stepped into the batter's box for the A's.

Like Johnson, he was a Bay Area native. In fact, he had faced Johnson a number of times in both high school and college. There was no other hitter in the major leagues with more experience hitting against Johnson.

No matter how well Johnson was pitching, Blankenship wasn't intimidated. He'd had plenty of hits against him before.

He ripped the second pitch through the infield for a solid base hit. The no-hitter was gone.

But Johnson was undeterred. He still had some work to do. After walking Rickey Henderson to load the bases, he went to work on Eric Fox.

Fox didn't have a chance. Johnson punched him out for his thirteenth strikeout of the game.

Now came Sierra, known as one of the best fastball hitters in baseball.

That didn't matter to Randy Johnson.

With two strikes, Sierra swung through a fastball for Johnson's fourteenth strikeout. As the pitch rocketed past Sierra, Johnson raised his arms in triumph and looked to the sky, then thumped his glove to his heart.

After the game he admitted, "I felt my father's presence. When I pointed up afterwards, it was for my dad. If I have a guardian angel, it's my father."

The victory set the tone for Johnson's season. He proved that his performance at the end of 1992 was no fluke.

He became one of the best pitchers in the game. His control, which had always been his Achilles' heel, now became his greatest ally. By getting ahead of the hitters early in the count, he got more strikeouts and threw fewer pitches. Now Johnson regularly pitched into the late innings of games. Each time he took the mound, he expected to pitch a complete game and win. Strikeouts weren't the object anymore, just something that happened along the way if he was pitching well.

"I'm not trying to strike everyone out," he explained to a reporter. "I'm pitching now. I've become a little more focused and a little more dedicated toward what I have to do since my father's death. He was a battler. I've tried to be like that.

"Nothing that happens on the field will ever discourage me again. I'll never say 'I can't handle it.' There's no situation I'll get into that I can't get out of. None."

Those words were bad news for hitters in the American League. At the All-Star break Johnson was 10–5. He was selected for the team for the second time in his career.

Before a capacity crowd at Camden Yards in Baltimore, Johnson gave baseball fans everywhere an enduring memory.

In the days preceding the game, Philadelphia Phillies outfielder John Kruk, a National League All-Star, had worried about facing Johnson. A left-handed-hitting batter, Kruk had seen Johnson pitch on television and didn't look forward to facing the most intimidating pitcher in baseball. Before the game he quipped "I haven't slept for the last two days."

When Kruk stepped in to face Johnson, he looked out at the big pitcher, gave a faint smile, then just started shaking his head. He couldn't believe a pitcher could be so big and scary looking.

Randy Johnson had his game face on. He narrowed his eyes and glared back at Kruk, trying to look as mean and nasty as possible. Kruk stepped back in the batter's box as far as he could.

The umpire signaled for Johnson to pitch. He took careful aim, wound up, and . . .

ZIP!

He threw the ball directly over Kruk's head! The ball rocketed against the backstop as Johnson scowled. Then he gave the joke away, allowing a faint smile to crease his lips.

Now Kruk started laughing as the crowd roared and laughed along. He looked like he had seen a ghost. He knew that Johnson hadn't tried to hit him, but had thrown the ball way over his head on purpose, partly to intimidate him, but more to entertain the crowd.

Still, Kruk wasn't taking any chances. As Johnson wound up to throw his next pitch Kruk again stood at the far back corner of the batter's box. When Johnson released the ball, he ducked away.

The ball streaked across the plate for a strike.

Kruk just started shaking his head. There was no way he could hit the ball.

As Johnson burned the next two pitches past him, Kruk managed two weak swings as he bailed out of the batter's box, missing each pitch by at least three feet for a strikeout. Johnson went on to pitch two scoreless innings.

After the game, Kruk joked that after the first pitch, "I was just glad to be alive. All I know is I don't want to face him again."

Johnson pretended the pitch was an accident and deadpanned, "Maybe you'd call that a setup pitch. With the heat and humidity, the ball was very slippery."

The incident made Johnson a household name to even casual baseball fans. Now, everyone paid attention when Randy Johnson pitched.

Incredibly, now the Mariners considered trading him. His newfound control made him attractive to other teams. Seattle was afraid they wouldn't be able to afford his next contract and entertained several trade possibilities, looking for young prospects in return, just as they themselves had done when they traded Mark Langston for Johnson.

The Toronto Blue Jays made an attractive offer. But on July 23, Johnson pitched his worst game of the year against Cleveland, giving up eight runs in one and a third innings. The Blue Jays backed off.

Johnson bounced back from that poor performance by pitching even better than before. He won nine of his last ten decisions, including his last eight. From August 14 through the end of the season, in 85 innings he struck out 107 and gave up only 55 hits and 25 walks.

He finished with a record of 19–8 as the Mariners finished above .500 for the first time ever, with a record of 82–80. In 255 innings he struck out 308. Best of all, he walked only 99. In batting-average allowed he led the majors, holding opponents to a mere .209.

In the off-season he was rewarded with a four-year contract worth $20 million. The Mariners had decided that they had to keep Randy Johnson.

With Ken Griffey Jr., outfielder Jay Buhner, first baseman Tino Martinez, and third baseman–DH Edgar Martinez in the lineup, the Mariners were emerging as one of the most exciting young teams in baseball. Entering the 1994 season, they expected to build upon their surprising performance in 1993 and challenge for the division title.

Baseball reorganized its divisional structure in 1994, creating a Central Division to go with the existing Eastern and Western Division in each league. The three division winners, plus a fourth team with the next best record, would make the playoffs, increasing the Mariners chances. They were matched with Texas, Oakland, and California in the AL West.

Yet for most of the season, it didn't appear as if any team in the division wanted to win the title. None was playing .500 baseball.

Once again, Randy Johnson kept the Mariners afloat. He was the only starting pitcher on the team that was doing his job.

By early August, the Mariners, despite being more than ten games below .500, were still in the race for the divisional title. They were only a game or two out of first place. Johnson was awesome. His twelve wins were fourth best in the league, while his 204 strikeouts led all of baseball. With a strong finish, the Mariners could still make the playoffs.

Johnson appeared up to the challenge. On August

11 he struck out fifteen hitters and won his thirteenth game. He was poised for a big finish.

But at midnight, every player in major league baseball went on strike over a disagreement with the baseball owners. Although the players and owners spent the next several weeks negotiating, both sides refused to budge. On September 14, the remainder of the season, including the World Series, was canceled.

There was nothing Randy Johnson could do but begin preparing for the 1995 season. He promised himself that he would spend the strike getting in the best condition of his career.

He did allow himself one distraction, however. On December 28 his wife, Lisa, gave birth to a daughter they named Samantha. Now that he was a father, Johnson found it even easier to remain focused on his goals.

The strike was finally settled late in the spring of 1995. But by the time the regular season started, three weeks late, there wasn't enough time to play a full schedule. As a result, the 1995 season lasted only 144 games instead of the full 162-game schedule that is standard in the major leagues.

Unlike many players, Randy Johnson was in mid-season form, ready to play hard.

Many baseball fans were slow to return to the game they felt had betrayed them with the strike. But soon, the Mariners stands were filled again. As a team, the Mariners were much improved. Tino Martinez, Edgar Martinez, and Jay Buhner all responded with career years at the plate, while starting pitchers Chris Bosio and Tim Belcher finally gave Randy some help on the mound.

Not that he needed much. The Big Unit was on automatic pilot all year long.

Only a few times in baseball history has a pitcher been as dominant as Randy Johnson was in 1995. Nearly every time he took the mound, he returned with a Mariners victory.

Hitters were all but helpless against him, batting just over .200. Nolan Ryan held the single-season mark of 11.48 strikeouts per game, set in 1987 in the National League. Johnson, who unlike Ryan had to pitch against the designated hitter in the American League, averaged nearly thirteen strikeouts a game.

Although the California Angels jumped out to a

big lead in the division when Ken Griffey Jr. had to leave the Mariners lineup with a broken wrist, Johnson single-handedly kept the team in the race. After falling to Minnesota in late June, Johnson simply refused to lose again.

Meanwhile, the California Angels started running out of steam. Though they led by as many as eleven games in mid-August, they collapsed as the Mariners, keyed by Johnson, surged. By the last week in the season, his record stood at 17–2. Moreover, in his twenty-nine starts, the Mariners were a stellar 26–3.

The two clubs finished the regular season tied for the divisional lead with identical 78–67 records. They met in Seattle on Sunday, October 1, in a one-game playoff to decide the AL West title.

To no one's surprise, the Mariners gave the ball to Randy Johnson. Despite the fact that he had only three days' rest instead of his usual four, the team needed him to pitch. Pitching for the Angels was, ironically enough, Mark Langston, with a record of 15–6.

The two pitchers both started out strongly, neither man giving up a run in the first two innings. But when the Rangers came to bat in the third, Johnson showed the Angels that he didn't intend to lose.

He struck out the side, then did it again in the fifth. In the bottom of the inning the Mariners finally scratched out a run to take a 1–0 lead.

Langston tired in the seventh, and Seattle exploded for four runs, then added four more in the eighth off a series of relief pitchers to take a commanding 9–0 lead as the Angels came to bat for the final time.

Only now did Johnson begin to relent. He allowed a leadoff home run to Tony Phillips. Then he settled down and retired the next two batters easily before ending the game with a flourish, striking out Tim Salmon for his twelfth strikeout of the day.

Randy Johnson looked to the sky, raised his arms, and pounded his glove against his chest. The message was clear. Johnson and the Mariners were going to the playoffs.

Chapter Nine
1995

The Pitcher

Few observers gave the Mariners much of a chance in the playoffs, which began just two days after the Mariners victory over the Angels. In the first round they were matched against the New York Yankees. Had Johnson been well rested, and available to pitch twice in the five-game series, everyone figured the Mariners might do all right. But with Johnson unavailable to pitch in either of the first two games, the Yankees looked like a sure bet.

The New York pitching staff was deep and experienced. Starting pitchers Jack McDowell and David Cone were both past winners of the Cy Young Award, which is given each year to the best pitcher in the league. Reliever John Wetteland was one of the best in baseball. On offense, New York was keyed by young star Bernie Williams and veterans

Wade Boggs and Don Mattingly. The Yankees, after compiling the best record in baseball during the strike-shortened 1994 season, were determined not to let this opportunity slip away.

Although Seattle's offense was just as strong, if not better than New York's, after Randy Johnson their pitching staff was a mystery. While starters Chris Bosio, Tim Belcher, and late-season pickup Andy Benes had all pitched well at times, they were inconsistent. The Mariners bullpen had struggled all year.

The five-game series started off predictably. Despite Ken Griffey Jr.'s two home runs, New York won Game One 9–6 by battering five Seattle pitchers. Game Two was a classic, as the two clubs went fifteen innings before New York's Jim Leyritz won it with a dramatic two-run homer to give the Yankees a 7–5 victory.

The Mariners were in trouble. New York needed only one more victory to advance to the league championship series against Cleveland.

The two teams traveled to Seattle for Game Three. Randy Johnson didn't even bother to ask the manager if he was going to pitch. He knew. If he didn't win, he had all winter to rest his arm.

But New York wasn't going to roll over and play dead for Johnson. In fact, they were one of the few clubs that had any success against him all year long. Besides, they were convinced that their pitcher, Jack McDowell, was every bit as tough as Johnson. Even though he didn't throw nearly as hard as Johnson, McDowell was known for his ability to win even when he wasn't throwing well. He simply never gave up.

Neither team scored during the first three innings. Then, in the top of the fourth, switch-hitting Bernie Williams turned on a Johnson slider and pulled it into the stands for a home run. New York led, 1–0.

In the fifth, the Mariners came back. Tino Martinez cracked a two-run homer to put Seattle ahead, 2–1. With Randy Johnson pitching with a lead, Seattle felt invincible.

They exploded for five more runs in the sixth to knock McDowell from the ball game and take a 7–1 lead. Johnson pitched through the seventh inning, recording his tenth strikeout, before turning the game over to the bullpen. Seattle held on to win, 7–4.

The victory energized the team. In Game Four, despite falling behind 5–0, they battled back behind Edgar Martinez's two home runs and seven RBIs to win going away, 11–8. They had tied the series. The winner of the next game would advance.

Before the Mariners took the field to start Game Five, Lou Piniella looked over at Randy Johnson and asked, "Are you good for a couple of batters?" Johnson nodded his head affirmatively.

Both teams' pitching had been worn thin by the hard-fought series. Who would follow starting pitchers David Cone for New York and Andy Benes for Seattle was anyone's guess.

The two teams battled back and forth all game long. New York nursed a two-run lead into the eighth before David Cone tired, giving up a home run to Griffey, then loading the bases and walking home the tying run.

But New York battled back in the top of the ninth. In relief of Benes, Norm Charlton opened the ninth by giving up a leadoff double to New York infielder Tony Fernandez. He then walked Randy Velarde.

Randy Johnson was up in the bullpen as soon as it was clear Charlton was in trouble. When the second batter reached base, Manager Lou Piniella strode to the mound and waved for Johnson.

The capacity crowd of 57,411 fans at the Seattle Kingdome stood and cheered as one as Johnson came out to pitch for the third time in only seven days. Yankee third baseman Wade Boggs stepped into the batter's box.

Johnson didn't waste time.

SMACK! he blew a fastball past Boggs as the crowd went nuts.

Then *ZIP!*

CRACK!

Two more pitches and Boggs went back to the dugout with a rare strikeout.

With the crowd cheering louder on each pitch, Johnson retired both Bernie Williams and Paul O'Neill on pop-ups. The game was still tied.

When the Mariners threatened in the bottom of the ninth, the Yankees brought back Jack McDowell. He squelched the rally by performing some strikeout magic on Edgar Martinez, then caused Alex Rodriguez to ground out. The game entered extra innings. Both teams pulled out all the stops in an effort to win.

In the top of the tenth, the Yankees sent Ruben Sierra, Don Mattingly, and Gerald Williams to the plate to face Johnson.

But Johnson had rarely been better. Pitching with his heart as much as his arm, he struck out all three men. In the bottom of the tenth, the Mariners threatened again, but McDowell worked his way out of the jam.

When Johnson took the mound at the top of the eleventh, Piniella knew it would be his last inning. He only hoped Johnson had enough for three more outs.

Johnson finally started showing his fatigue, and walked catcher Mike Stanley on four pitches. Stanley was sacrificed to second, then Randy Velarde, who had nineteen hits in forty career at bats against Johnson, singled up the middle. New York led, 5–4.

On the bench, Piniella didn't move. The Mariners

were either going to win or lose with Randy Johnson. There was one out.

Summoning the last of his strength, Johnson concentrated on the dangerous pinch hitter Jim Leyritz. In Game Two, his fifteenth-inning home run had won the game for New York.

But Randy Johnson would not be denied. He struck him out.

He then pitched carefully to Bernie Williams. He didn't want Williams to pull another home run. Williams walked.

Now came Paul O'Neill. The left-handed-hitting outfielder didn't have a chance. Johnson blew three pitches past him, and the Mariners were out of the inning. As Johnson walked from the mound, completely spent, the Kingdome erupted in cheers.

Riding a wave of emotion, the Mariners bats struck back. Joey Cora opened the inning with a bunt single, then went to third when Griffey followed with a base hit.

With men on first and third, Edgar Martinez stepped to the plate. All year long he had responded in similar situations with a big hit.

He did so again, smacking McDowell's offering down the left-field line. Cora scored easily and the speedy Griffey started running and didn't stop until he slid across home plate, giving Seattle a 6–5 win and earning them the right to face Cleveland in the league championship series. Randy Johnson — who else? — was the winning pitcher.

The exhausted Mariners moved on to face Cleveland for the American League pennant. When Randy Johnson won Game Three, the underdog Mariners led the Indians two games to one.

Then the Mariners ran out of miracles. Cleveland stormed back to win the next two games to enter Game Six needing only one more win to reach the World Series.

One final time, the Mariners called on Randy Johnson.

For the fourth time in only three weeks, he took the mound with less than his accustomed four days' rest. Once again, it was time for Johnson to be a warrior.

This time his fastball didn't crackle across the plate at ninety-seven or ninety-eight mph. He was too tired and too sore to throw that hard.

But he was a pitcher, not a thrower. He depended on his slider and change-up, utilizing his experience to keep the Indians off balance. With experience at his back, Johnson knew that a successful pitcher uses his brain as much as his arm.

Yet as he kept the Indians off balance, Cleveland pitcher Orel Hershiser shut down the Mariners. Then Johnson's defense fell apart, as the Indians scored two in the fifth on Cora's throwing error, and two more in the eighth when catcher Dan Wilson failed to handle a Johnson slider. Trailing 4–0, Johnson reluctantly left the field as everyone in the Kingdome stood and cheered, not just for the way he had pitched that night, but for the way he had pitched all year long, each and every time he took the mound. On the Indians bench, even pitcher Orel Hershiser stood and applauded.

Two innings later, the Indians won the American League pennant and the right to play the Atlanta Braves in the World Series.

After the game, Randy Johnson tried to be philosophical. "Our season came to an end tonight, but I don't think anybody in this locker room should be upset," he said. "Nobody expected us to get this far."

Then he just shook his head. "I'm only human," he said with a sigh. "I'm not making excuses, but I was getting tired. The last two weeks have been very draining."

Then he paused a moment before he spoke again. "I think the most important thing is everybody in this locker room knows how to win now, and most of us didn't know that before the season began."

If they did now, it was because Randy Johnson had showed them.

Chapter Ten
1996–1997

The Big Unit's Comeback

At the end of the 1995 season, Johnson was exhausted. But at the same time, he was deeply satisfied. He knew that he had pitched as well as he could for as long as he could. By pitching without enough rest in the playoffs, he had risked injury, and thus his own future, for the good of the team.

His performance won him the respect of every player and fan in the country. With an 18–2 record, his .900 winning percentage led the American League, as did his 294 strikouts and 2.48 ERA. For the season, he averaged 12.35 strikeouts per nine innings, the best single-season mark ever. To no one's surprise, in the off-season he was named the winner of the Cy Young Award as the best pitcher in the American League.

He was happy with his life, and he made good

on his promise to himself to do what he could to help others. He put out a calendar featuring his photographs that benefited the homeless, built a baseball clubhouse for his old high school, and contributed to a number of other charities.

When Randy arrived at spring training in March of 1996, he was more confident of his ability than ever before. When writers started to talk to him about his amazing record in 1995, Randy usually cut them off and said, "I can get better."

He received more good news just as the season opened. His wife, Lisa, gave birth to their second child, a son. They named the boy Tanner Rolen, after Randy's father.

Johnson began the 1996 season exhibiting the same dominance he had in 1995. He won his first several starts and looked forward to yet another record-breaking season.

But in Milwaukee on April 26, Johnson's lower back began hurting him. He left the game as a precautionary measure in the fourth inning.

After resting for a few days, the back felt better. On May 1, he made his next start against Texas.

This time he lasted only two innings before lifting

himself from the game, this time because of a tight muscle in his leg. His back had also started hurting again.

He skipped a start, and didn't return to the rotation until May 12. He pitched five innings to collect his fifth win of the year and twelfth regular-season victory in a row. But he left the game in excruciating pain.

His lower back was killing him, and sending sharp pain down his legs. Although few of his teammates knew, playing baseball the past few weeks had been pure agony for Johnson. In between innings he had actually been going back to the clubhouse and lying down on the floor, trying to keep his back muscles from going into spasm.

He couldn't keep the pain a secret anymore. On May 15, the Mariners put Randy on the disabled list and sent him to see a doctor.

He was diagnosed with a bulging disk in his lower back. Since back surgery is sometimes risky, they put Johnson on a rehabilitation program, trying to build up his back strength while also allowing him to rest and heal.

In early August, Johnson decided it was time to

try to pitch again. Without him, the Mariners were floundering. Although his back still hurt, he felt as if he owed it to his teammates to try to pitch. He thought he'd be able to push the pain from his mind, at least for a few months. That would be just long enough, he hoped, to get the Mariners through the World Series.

He made one rehabilitation start in the minor leagues then rejoined Seattle on August 6. He pitched out of the bullpen and the Mariners hoped he would slowly build up his stamina and strength.

But after making only six appearances, Johnson had to stop pitching. His back was absolutely killing him. It was all he could do to get out of a chair or lift himself from bed, much less pitch. The Mariners put him back on the disabled list.

Johnson and the team doctors now decided that surgery was his only option. They diagnosed his condition as an "extruded disc herniation." On September 11, Johnson underwent surgery in Los Angeles. Doctors removed the disk, hoping that by doing so, they would relieve pressure on the nerves that caused Johnson so much pain. His season was over.

So was the Mariners'. Paced by their twenty-year-old shortstop, Alex Rodriguez, who hit .355 and smacked thirty-six home runs, their offense kept them in the race. But without Johnson, they simply didn't have enough pitching to win. Still, they finished only four and a half games back of the first-place Texas Rangers with a record of 85–76.

Randy Johnson didn't know what to think. The surgery was designed to help his pain. The doctors couldn't promise him that he would be able to pitch again.

After leaving the hospital he had to rest quietly for three weeks before he was allowed to begin a rehabilitation program. That was probably the hardest part for Johnson. Sitting around doing nothing for three weeks drove him nuts.

When he was given the green light by his doctors, he slowly tried to build up his back while at the same time resuming his usual off-season conditioning program. He discovered that he had to learn how to do some of the most commonplace activities, like picking up his daughter and son, in entirely new ways, all in order to keep his back from going out again.

The slow pace of his recovery frustrated him. "It's

been an emotional roller coaster," he admitted to the press. Every once in a while, he was still bothered by a burning sensation that ran down his legs all the way to his toes. Just a few weeks before the start of spring training, after he had begun working out on an exercise bike again, the pain returned and Johnson had to back off his program. He began to wonder if he would ever be able to pitch again.

Doctors told him that the problem didn't happen all at once. Rather, it was the product of years of wear and tear on his back. Because Randy was so tall, he didn't use his legs to provide power as much as other pitchers. His back took on the strain. After throwing thousands and thousands of pitches, it had simply given out. In order to pitch again, he would have to make his back even stronger than it was before the injury, to compensate for the missing disk.

During spring training 1997, he worked out at his own pace. It was up to him to tell the Mariners when he felt healthy enough to pitch again.

He started slowly, limiting himself to just a couple

of innings and a couple dozen pitches in his first few exhibition appearances, before building up to five innings by the end of spring training.

The results weren't particularly encouraging. Johnson ended the preseason with a 1–1 record and a 5.06 ERA. Of more concern were the ten walks he gave up in only sixteen innings of work.

Although his doctors cautioned him that his recovery would take time, Johnson was impatient. It didn't help when the season started and he struggled in his first few starts. Although he still managed to win, he wasn't the same dominant pitcher he had been before the surgery.

On May 2, he finally had a breakthrough. Against the Milwaukee Brewers, he pitched eight strong innings, giving up only three hits and striking out eleven. Johnson was cautiously optimistic.

But in his next start, against Baltimore on May 6, Johnson appeared to be in command when the game was delayed by a rain shower. When he returned to the mound, he was hit hard and suffered his first defeat in sixteen regular-season decisions stretching back to August of 1994.

Ten days later, he lost to the Orioles again. After the game, he told doctors his back and arm felt stiff.

They weren't nearly as concerned as Johnson was. They told him he would have to expect some discomfort.

Johnson had to take extra precautions to take care of his back. In between innings, instead of sitting on the bench, he returned to the clubhouse and lay down with his feet elevated in order to take the strain off his back. After each game he lay facedown for an hour on a special table also designed to take the strain off his back. Then the team trainer packed his body in ice from his neck to his feet.

Finally, in late May, Johnson's improving condition allowed him to return to form. In a game against Texas, he suddenly felt comfortable again. Against a powerful Rangers lineup, his fastball was regularly timed at ninety-seven and ninety-eight miles per hour. He struck out fifteen, and pitched the Mariners to a 5–0 victory.

"The last time I was dominating like that and got that tired was in high school," quipped Johnson, "when I scored fifty-one points in a basketball game."

Johnson's opponents soon wished he were back in school. He was more than back. Somehow, he was actually better. His spring-training prediction of two years before was coming true.

In late June, he pitched one of the most remarkable games of his career. In a complete game against the Oakland A's, Johnson struck out nineteen hitters, a new record for a lefty. By a whisker, he missed tying Roger Clemens's record.

Yet despite the high number of strikeouts, the A's got to Johnson. He gave up a total of eleven hits.

People still talk about one particular hit. Late in the game, Johnson looked in at A's slugger Mark McGwire.

Perhaps no hitter in the major leagues is as feared as McGwire. Over the course of his career he has hit home runs more frequently than any other active player. Not only that, but he hits the ball farther than most. Johnson versus McGwire is a contest of power against power. Randy stared down at McGwire, took the sign, then threw the slugger a ninety-eight-mile-per-hour fastball.

McGwire guessed at the speed and location of the

pitch and swung as hard as he could. The ball rocketed from his bat at lightning speed.

Then it just kept going. The ball looked as if it might never come down again as the fans at the Oakland Coliseum looked on in amazement.

Finally the ball clattered against some empty seats far back in the upper deck in left center field. No one had ever hit a ball that far in Oakland before.

McGwire's home run was estimated to have traveled 538 feet, one of the longest home runs ever recorded. The A's won, 4–1.

Reporters expected Johnson to be happy with his performance after the game. He wasn't.

"I really don't care about the strikeouts," he said, although he admitted it would be nice to tie Clemens's record. "I'd give up all the strikeouts for a win. You might not believe it, but that's all I really care about."

A few weeks later Johnson was again named to the American League All-Star team. All-Star manager Joe Torre of the New York Yankees chose Randy to start the game for the American League.

This time, it wasn't John Kruk but outfielder Larry Walker of the Colorado Rockies who worried about facing Johnson. Earlier in the year, in an interleague game between the Mariners and Rockies, Walker, despite the fact that he was hitting well over .400 at the time, chose to sit out the game, rather than bat against Johnson. The press joked that he was ill with "Johnsonitis," and he was widely criticized. He knew he couldn't avoid Johnson now.

When Walker stepped in to face the Big Unit, like Kruk several years before, he dug in far back in the batter's box.

Johnson wound up and threw.

The pitch sailed over Walker's head as he ducked to the ground!

He got up laughing, hardly able to believe that Johnson had thrown the same pitch to him that he had thrown to Kruk in the '93 All-Star game. Then Walker, smiling widely, put his batting helmet on backwards, turned around, and stepped into the right-handed-hitting batter's box.

Now it was Johnson's turn to smile. He pitched carefully, and eventually walked Walker. That night and the next day, their memorable confrontation was shown on highlight reels all over the country. Even though both are among the best players in the game, they know how to have fun.

As the 1997 season drew to a close, Randy Johnson still had one more remarkable game in his equally remarkable left arm.

On August 8, against the Chicago White Sox, Johnson again flirted with history, striking out nineteen hitters for the second time in one season. No pitcher had ever done that before. And this time, Randy Johnson won the game.

Johnson appeared poised to lead the Mariners to the World Series. But on August 20, while pitching against Cleveland, he was forced to leave the game with a sore finger on his left hand.

He still won the game, 1–0, to improve his record to 17–4, but the finger hurt so much he couldn't throw. The team doctor diagnosed the injury as tendinitis.

Randy missed four starts while the finger healed, and the injury probably cost him any chance he had to win another Cy Young Award, which later went to Toronto Blue Jays pitcher Roger Clemens. Fortunately, while Johnson was out of the lineup the

Mariners played well and wrapped up the American League Western Division championship.

Randy returned to the lineup in mid-September, and while he pitched well, collecting his eighteenth and nineteenth wins of the season, he wasn't quite as dominant as he had been before the injury. He really wanted to win twenty games, but the regular season was just about over and Randy wasn't scheduled to make another start. The Mariners wanted him to be well rested for the playoffs.

But Mariners manager Lou Piniella understood how important twenty wins is for a major league pitcher. On September 27, in the next-to-the-last game of the regular season, Seattle led Oakland 7–1 after four innings.

Piniella pulled starter Omar Olivares and put Randy into the game as a relief pitcher. Since a starting pitcher must pitch at least five innings to be eligible for the win, Johnson became the pitcher of record.

He threw two shutout innings. The Mariners held on to win, 9–3, and Johnson captured his twentieth victory of the season. Now he could focus on the playoffs.

Seattle faced the Eastern Division champion Baltimore Orioles in the first-round best-of-five American League division series. To no one's surprise, Randy was named starting pitcher for the first game on October 1.

But the Orioles had given Randy trouble all year long, and they did so again in the playoffs. He and Oriole starter Mike Mussina battled to a 1–1 tie through four innings. Then the Orioles exploded for four fifth-inning runs. Randy left the game without getting anyone out in the sixth, and Seattle lost, 9–3.

The Mariners got more bad news the next day. Early in Game Two of the playoffs, Jamie Moyer, the Mariners second-best pitcher, hurt his arm. He left the game and the Orioles won 9–3 once more to go ahead in the series two games to none.

It would be tough for the Mariners to come back and win the series, but they tried, defeating Baltimore in Game Three on October 4, 4–2.

The next day, the Mariners again turned to Randy Johnson. In a rematch of Game One, he would face the Orioles ace, Mike Mussina.

Both pitched great. Johnson gave up only seven hits and struck out thirteen Orioles. Leadoff batter

Brady Anderson struck out all four times he came to bat!

But two of the seven hits off Randy were home runs, allowing the Orioles to score three runs.

Unfortunately for Johnson, Mike Mussina pitched even better than he did, striking out nine Mariners and giving up only two hits and one run in seven innings before turning the game over to the Orioles bullpen. They shut down the Mariners, and Baltimore won, 3–1, to take the division series. Randy Johnson's and the Seattle Mariners' season was over.

At age thirty-four, Johnson is in his prime. To many, he is considered the equal of any great fastball pitcher who has ever played the game, from Walter Johnson to Sandy Koufax, Nolan Ryan, and Roger Clemens.

Yet as remarkable as he is as a pitcher, Johnson is perhaps even more admirable for the way he has learned to control himself, and, by hard work and determination, to reach the goal he set for himself while he was still an awkward Little Leaguer throwing a tennis ball against his father's garage.

"I'm not going to say I'm the best pitcher," he says today. "But I would like to think that my hard work and competitiveness have allowed me to be among the best. But not the best."

That's bad news for hitters everywhere. For as Randy Johnson has proven over and over again, he just keeps getting better.

MATT CHRISTOPHER

The #1 Sports Writer for Kids

Read them all!